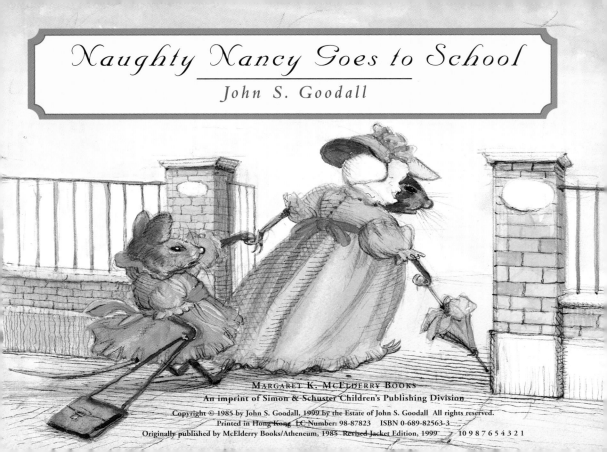

Naughty Nancy Goes to School

John S. Goodall

MARGARET K. MCELDERRY BOOKS
An imprint of Simon & Schuster Children's Publishing Division

Printed in Hong Kong LC Number: 98-87823   ISBN 0-689-82563-3
Originally published by McElderry Books/Atheneum, 1985 Revised Jacket Edition, 1999   10 9 8 7 6 5 4 3 2 1

SCHOOL
NOTICE

NANCY THE VALIANT
WE LOVE YOU.